Five Little Firefighters

Tom Graham

Henry Holt and Company ★ New York

Henry Holt and Company, LLC
Publishers since 1866
175 Fifth Avenue
New York, New York 10010
www.HenryHoltKids.com

Library of Congress Cataloging-in-Publication Data
Graham, Thomas.
Five little firefighters / story and pictures by Tom Graham.—1st ed.
p.   cm.
Summary: Even though their dinner is ready to eat, when the fire alarm bell
sounds, the firefighters must go out to rescue a family and their cat.
ISBN-13: 978-0-8050-8697-3 / ISBN-10: 0-8050-8697-8
[1. Fire fighters—Fiction. 2. Rescues—Fiction.] I. Title.
PZ7.G7579Fi 2008   [E]—dc22   2007040769

First Edition—2008 / Designed by Véronique Lefèvre Sweet
The artist digitally enhanced traditional watercolor paintings
on Canson paper to create the illustrations for this book.
Printed in the United States of America on acid-free paper. ∞
1 3 5 7 9 10 8 6 4 2

The five little firefighters are about to eat dinner when...

RRIIIINGGG!

They race to the fire engine.

EEEE-OOOHHH, EEEE-OOOHHH, HOONNKK!
EEEE-OOOHHH, EEEE-OOOHHH, HOONNKK!

The fire engine races and roars through the streets.

There are flames everywhere!

The five little firefighters get to work.

I've got him!

They rescue the baby.

Now everyone is safe!

It's time to go back to the firehouse.

At last the five little firefighters have their dinner.

Let's eat!

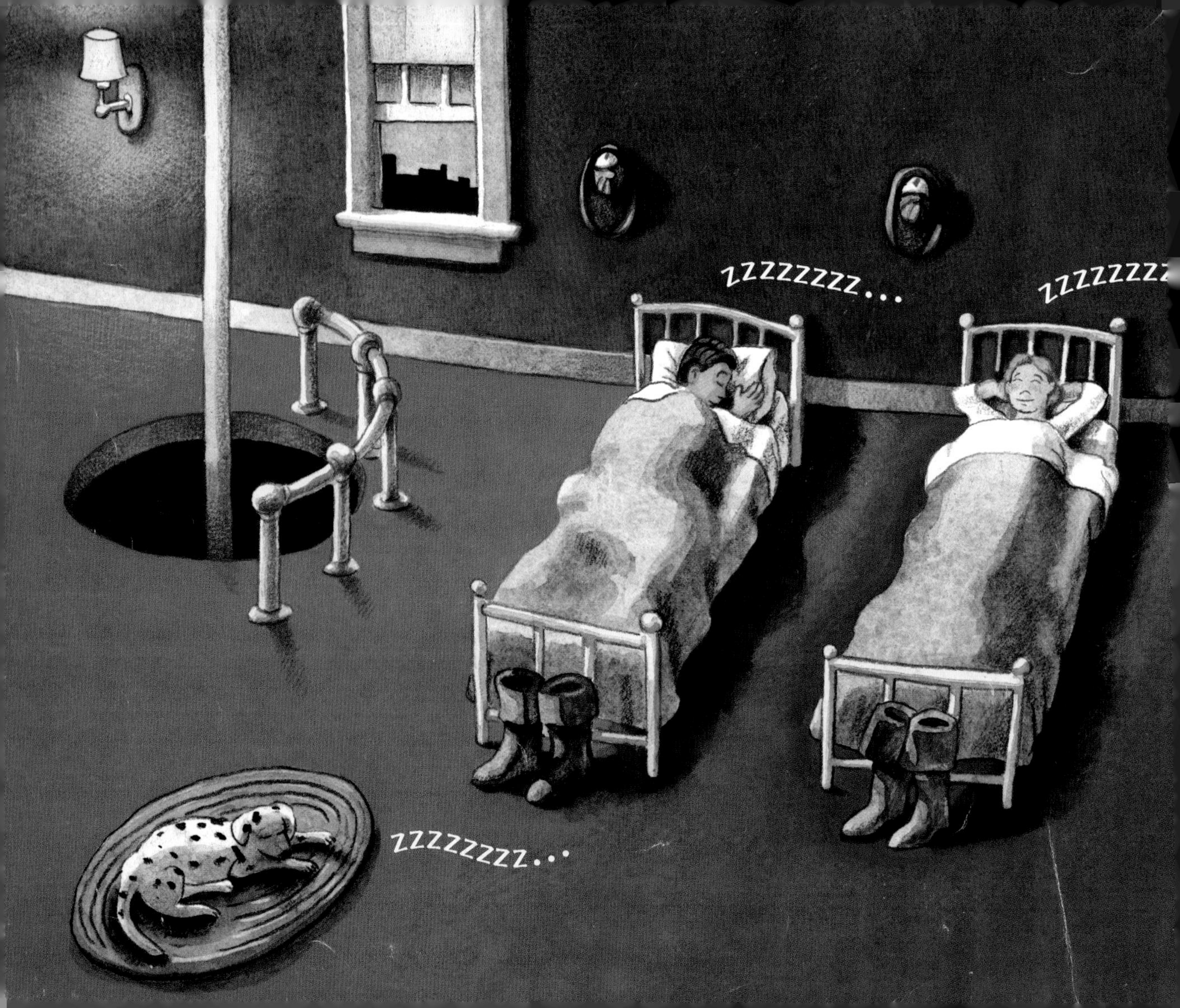
zzzzzzzz...
zzzzzzzz
zzzzzzzz...

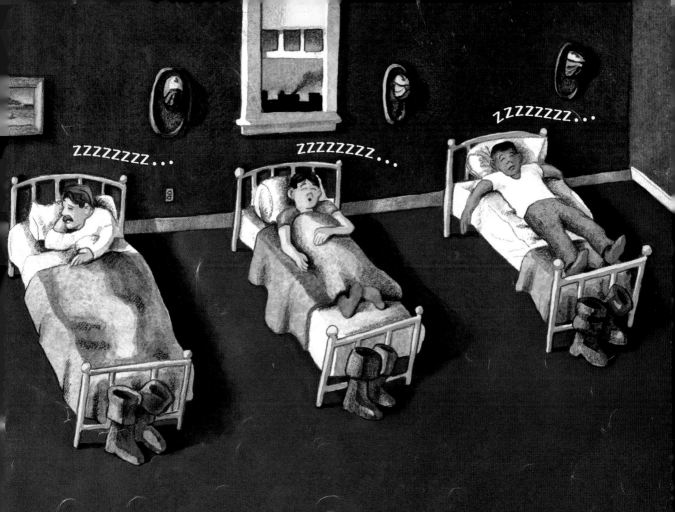